A Book of Mormon Story

I Will
GO
I Will
DO

To Marion Christenson, a teacher with great
faith and even greater patience.

Special Thanks to
Kathy Jenkins and Margaret Weber
for seeing and believing.

Other books by
TONI SORENSON:

Behold Your Little Ones

I Can't Go to Church

Heroes of the Book of Mormon

Heroes of the Bible

He Knows Your Heart: Inspiring Thoughts for Women

Redemption Road

Master

All photographs © Toni Sorenson
Cover and book design by Jessica Warner

Published by Covenant Communications, Inc., American Fork, Utah

Copyright © 2008 by Toni Sorenson

All rights reserved. No part of this work may be reproduced by any means without the express
written permission of Covenant Communications, Inc., P.O. Box 416, American Fork, UT
84003. This work is not an official publication of The Church of Jesus Christ of Latter-day
Saints. The views expressed within this work are the sole responsibility of the author and do not
necessarily reflect the position of The Church of Jesus Christ of Latter-day Saints, Covenant
Communications, Inc., or any other entity.

Printed in China
First Printing: September 2008
14 13 12 11 10 09 08   10 9 8 7 6 5 4 3 2 1

ISBN-13: 978-1-59811-627-4
ISBN-10: 1-59811-627-4

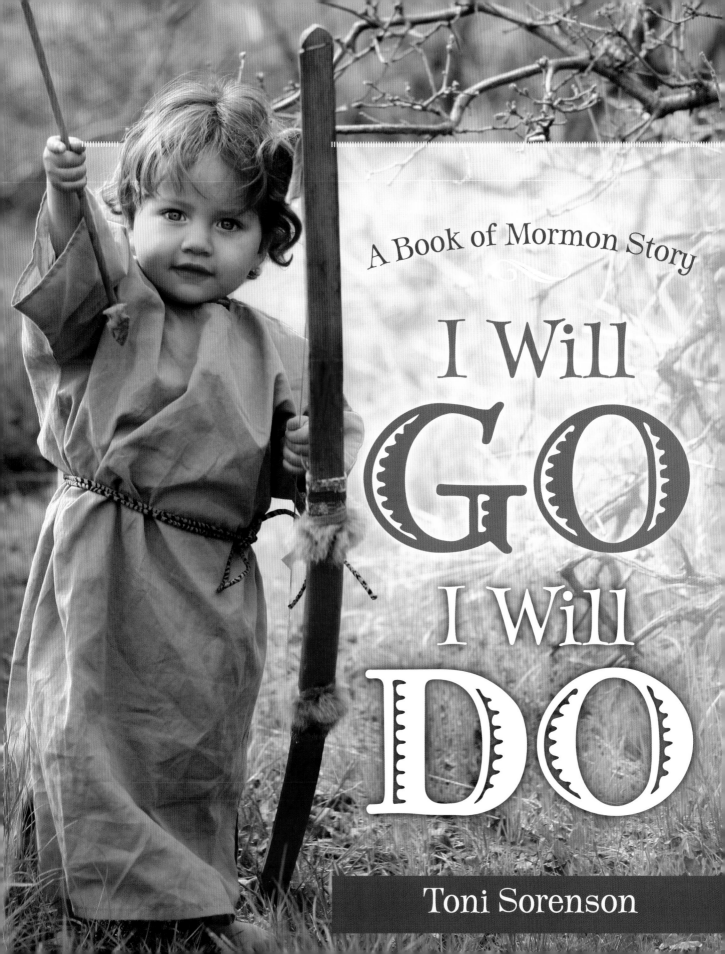

A Book of Mormon Story

I Will
GO
I Will
DO

Toni Sorenson

Nephi lived a long time ago in a city called Jerusalem. His father, Lehi, was a prophet.

The people of Jerusalem were wicked and did not keep the Lord's commandments.

The Lord commanded Lehi to move his family to a better place called the Promised Land. Lehi asked his sons to help get ready for the move.

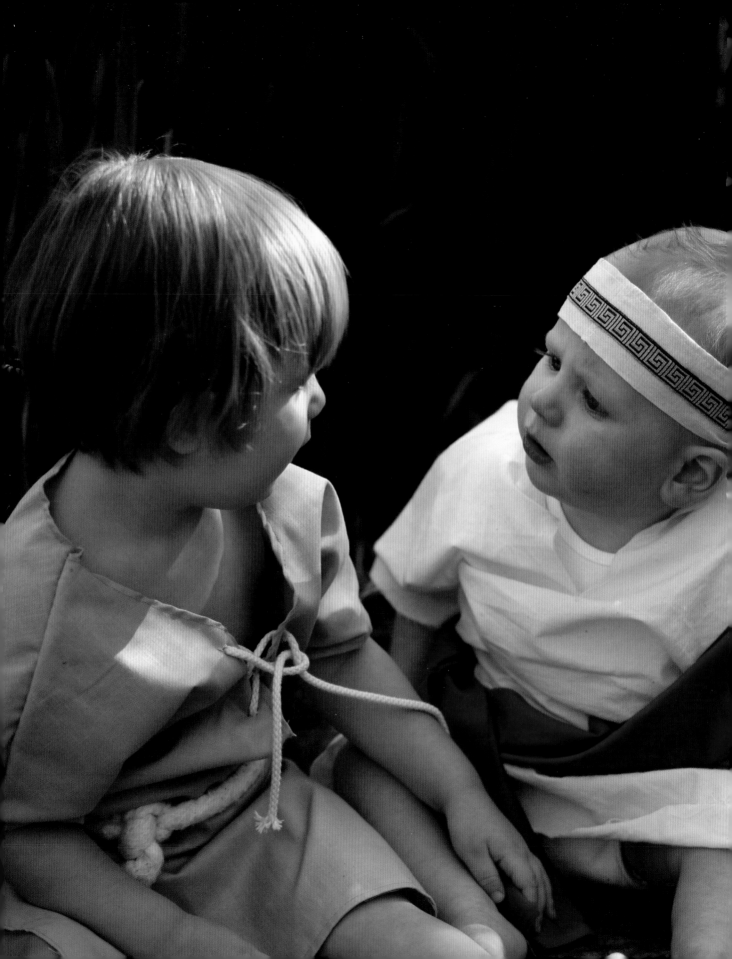

Two of Nephi's older brothers, Laman and Lemuel, did not want to move. They felt angry and murmured a lot.

Nephi decided he would always do the things the Lord commanded.

Ishmael was one of Lehi's closest friends. Ishmael and his daughters joined Lehi's family on their journey.

Nephi and his brothers were commanded to go back to Jerusalem to get some very special plates.

The plates were like a book that taught about Jesus and all of the Lord's commandments.

Laman and Lemuel did not want to go back to get the plates, but Nephi wanted to obey.

So did his brother, Sam.

All of the boys did go
back to Jerusalem to try
to get the plates, but the
journey back was hard and
dangerous. Sariah, their
mother, prayed for them.

A wicked man named Laban was in charge of the plates. He would not give them up, even when Nephi gave him treasure.

Nephi knew that getting the plates was a commandment. He told his brothers, "I will go and do the thing which the Lord hath commanded." Nephi knew that if the Lord commanded it, the Lord would provide a way for him to obey. He put on Laban's armor and was able to get the plates.

Nephi and his brothers returned safely to their family, but living in the wilderness was not easy. One time the family was hungry, and they could not find any food. Nephi and his brothers hunted for food with bows and arrows.

While he was hunting, Nephi's bow broke. He prayed to Heavenly Father for help. Instead of murmuring like the others, Nephi made a new bow, and he found food for the family.

As Nephi grew, he studied the commandments. When the Lord commanded Nephi to build a ship to sail to the Promised Land, he went to work and started to build. The Lord gave Nephi strength and courage. But Laman and Lemuel were angry. They did not want to help Nephi build the ship and they made fun of him for trying.

Finally, Nephi told his brothers that the Lord commanded they do this.

They said they would help Nephi build the boat. Their family sailed across the sea to the Promised Land.

The Lord commanded Nephi to make a record of all that happened. He made very special plates and on them he wrote his testimony. Even when Nephi's brothers fought with him, Nephi still tried to keep the commandments. The Lord showed him many things and gave him many blessings because he obeyed.

When we read the Book of Mormon today, we can read Nephi's testimony and the story of his family. We can see that the only way to be happy and blessed is to do the things the Lord commands.